A Gift To

~

_____

From

~

_____

First published 2012 by Fast-Print Publishing of Peterborough, England.

FastPrint
Publishing

THE WICKED WITCH OF THE WOODS
Copyright © Peter Wadsworth 2012

ISBN: 978-178035-481-1

The right of Peter Wadsworth to be identified as the author of this work has been asserted by him in
accordance with the Copyright, Designs and Patents Act 1988 and any subsequent amendments thereto.

A catalogue record for this book is available from the British Library

This book is for Seren

With many,many thanks to my young reviewers:

Freya(10), Eden(14), Catherine(11), Emily(10), Rebecca(11), Ruben(10) and Phoebe(13)

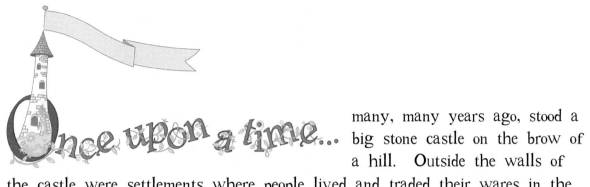

many, many years ago, stood a big stone castle on the brow of a hill. Outside the walls of the castle were settlements where people lived and traded their wares in the marketplace. Further out from the houses were thick, dense woods which went on for miles and miles, and were so dense that only a few of the townspeople ever ventured into them.

The people inside the castle, however, the King and Queen and all the courtiers, would use the woods for hunting and would ride their horses swiftly into the woods making lots of noise as they hunted for deer and boar.

But there was an even denser part of the woods that even they didn't venture into. It was so dense that not even the light of the sun could shine through the tree tops, making the whole area dark, cold and damp. This is where the Wicked-Witch-of-the-Woods lived. Very few people had seen the witch but there were many rumours as to all the evil things she could do. It was best to stay away from that part of the woods altogether.

That was true for all the people in the castle and for all the people outside the castle, but not for one little girl, aged five, who did not understand the rumours and who thought no one could be that evil. Her name was Emilia and she was the daughter of the King and Queen, a Princess in fact.

Princess Emilia was a pretty little girl with blonde, curly hair but she was stubbornly independent. She would wander around the castle alone having lost her chaperone by hiding in the many nooks and crannies of the castle. She would look out of the castle windows and wonder what it was like in the village and in the woods beyond. She would sigh because she was never allowed outside the castle walls.

Emilia was a determined little girl, so determined that she decided to go to the woods alone, to see the world beyond the castle walls. One day, she slipped her chaperone by hiding behind a large, stone column in the castle and made her way to the castle drawbridge, wearing a coat with a hood to hide her face. The sentries did not recognize her and she was allowed to pass through the castle gates.

Having looked around the village shops and market, and satisfied her curiosity, Emilia headed off towards the woods. It was a bright, sunny day, but suddenly, as she walked further into the woods, it became dark and cold and damp. Emilia had walked for a long time and now she was lost. She did not know the way back to the castle. She began to cry and buttoned her coat and hood ever more tightly to keep out the cold.

Emilia wiped away her tears and looked around her for something to eat. She was very hungry. She had eaten her breakfast but now her tummy was rumbling and she thought of all the very nice food in the castle. It was then, as she was looking for something to eat, that she noticed smoke coming from a little wooden house. As she approached the house, she could see the smoke from a chimney curling its way to the sky, suggesting a nice bright warm fire. She went to knock on the front door, either side of which was a brightly lit window. It made the house very inviting to a five-year-old.

Emilia knocked on the door but there was no answer. She knocked a second time and there was still no answer. She was about to knock a third time when she noticed the door was ajar. She pushed it, and it opened with a large creak. She went inside.

Emilia looked around and saw a large log fire and in the windows were two candle lamps lighting up the whole room. To one side of the house was a large wooden bench with bread and cake and, on a shelf nearby, many jars of different sizes and colours containing many strange and weird things. She shivered at the thought of what they might contain.

Having satisfied herself that there was no one at home, she settled into the rocking chair beside the fire and warmed her toes and hands. She took off her coat and hood and warmed the rest of her body. Glancing around the house, once again, the food on the table looked very inviting. She jumped out of the rocking chair and, using a stool to stand on, she took a knife out of one of the drawers and cut herself a large slice of bread.   Using a large forK, she toasted the bread in front of the fire.

It smelled delicious.   She went to the table again to looK for some butter but she couldn't find any.   Instead, to her surprise, she noticed a half-filled jar of jam.   She read the label:

Wild Blueberry Jam

her favourite, her very, very favourite jam, even more than strawberry jam.   With a large spoon she heaped the jam on her toast and smoothed it with the Knife.

Sitting back in the rocking chair in front of the fire, she ate the toast and jam hungrily.
It was delicious, simply delicious.
So delicious that she decided to have a second slice of jam on toast.

Having eaten the second slice, she sat back in the rocking chair and the warmth of the fire made her feel dozy and she closed her eyes and went into a deep, pleasant sleep.

Emilia woke up with a start by a hand shaking her shoulder. The hand had long, bony fingers and green-painted, long fingernails.

"Wake up! Wake up!" said a squeaky sort of voice.

Emilia rubbed her eyes and looked up at the face staring down at her. It was a funny-looking sort of face; it had a long, pointy nose with a small pair of spectacles balanced on the end of it; it had a long, thin chin and dark green eyes; it had lips painted the same colour of green as her fingernails.

Emilia jumped off the chair and looked at the figure in front of her. The woman was dressed in a long black gown, a green cape to keep warm, and a large black pointy, 5-sided hat with a large brim and a small green woollen bobble at the top. Everything about her was black and green. Emilia glanced at her feet and yes, of course, a pair of pointy green shoes. On the one hand the figure was frightening but, on the other hand, she didn't look all bad.

"Are you a witch?" asked Emilia, looking up at the tall figure.

"Some call me that," replied the witch.

"Are you the Wicked-Witch-of-the Woods?"

"Some call me that," repeated the witch.

The witch looked around the room and noticed the bread had been cut. "Was that you?" squeaked the witch, jabbing a pointy finger at Emilia.

"I was hungry and helped myself to some toast. You don't mind do you?"

"No, I don't mind," squeaked the witch and went over to the table to inspect the loaf of bread.

"Aaaaaargh!" shrieked the witch as loud as she could, the sound sending shivers of fear down Emilia's back.

"Aaaaaargh!" screamed the witch again, even louder, making Emilia's hairs on the back of her neck stand to attention.

The screams were so loud they had probably frightened all the animals and roosting birds in the wood.

"You have eaten my wild blueberry jam," screamed the witch again, holding the jar to the candlelight to see if there was any jam left. "You have eaten all of my jam, my precious jam, my favourite jam. That was the last jar and now I have to wait twelve months before I can make some more."

"Are you mad at me?" asked Emilia. "Are you going to cast a spell on me?"

"Of course not, my dear," said the witch in a much calmer voice, "of course not, that only happens in fairy tales."

The witch lied, because that's what witches do.

The witch went over to a big, very big book in one corner of the room. She blew the dust off its cover and cleaned it further with a green handkerchief. She adjusted her spectacles to the very tip of her nose and looked carefully at the 'Contents' page. Her bony finger ran down the page.

"Ah! Just what I thought," whispered the witch to herself, pointing to a section on 'Little girls who steal blueberry jam'. She hurriedly turned the large pages and noted the possible spells.

"Ah!" she repeated. "That's the one, that's the one."

Turning to Emilia with a forced smile on her green lips, she asked the little girl, "Would you like a hot cup of chocolate?"

"Oh, yes please," said Emilia. Hot chocolate was her favourite drink.

"Sit yourself in front of the fire dearie and I'll make you a nice cup of hot chocolate." The witch spoke in a nice, quiet voice.

Emilia sat on the chair in front of the fire and looked at the burning logs and flames which gave off a soft gentle glow. The witch, noticing Emilia wasn't watching her, set about making the chocolate. First the chocolate and hot milk, and then a special mix of frogs' legs, ground down into a paste, and other ingredients too foul to mention, were added to the chocolate.

"Drink this, my dear," said the witch, handing Emilia a green, pointy cup of chocolate. "It will make you nice and warm inside."

Emilia loved hot chocolate and drank every drop of it whilst the witch looked on with an evil smile on her face.

Suddenly, there were thumps on the front door, startling both Emilia and the witch. The door was flung open and two burly soldiers from the castle entered. They grabbed Emilia and scolded the witch. "You're lucky," bellowed one of the soldiers pointing to the witch, "that you haven't harmed the child, otherwise we are under orders to arrest you and put you in the castle dungeon."

"I'm fine," said Emilia, "the witch has looked after me and protected me from the cold outside. She has given me food and a cup of hot chocolate."

"Very well," said the soldier looking once again at the witch, "but let this be a lesson to you."

"Come on, said the other soldier to Emilia, "we are under orders to escort you back to the castle. The King and Queen have been frantic not

Knowing where you were. Grab your coat and come with us."

Emilia left with the soldiers and turned and waved goodbye to the witch. The witch waved back, with a huge smirk on her face.

~

Ten years have passed since that day. Princess Emilia was now fifteen-years-old and engaged to a handsome Prince, their marriage to be in two months' time.

The Princess should be happy, very happy, but she was not. Why? Ever since that day with the Wicked-Witch-of-the-Woods she could guess every present that was given to her. She knew, just by glancing at the box, what was inside it. She couldn't be surprised and that made her sad, very sad. She loved surprises, she always had, and now that pleasure in life had been taken away from her by the witch's spell.

Because Princess Emilia was sad, the Prince was sad, the King and Queen were sad, and all the courtiers were sad. No one knew what to do. Every time someone gave her a present she would guess instantly what was inside the box. Big boxes, little boxes, heavy boxes, light boxes, presents of all shapes and sizes. Nobody could surprise her any more.

The King, seeing how upset his daughter was before her wedding, summoned the wisest men in the land to the castle to break the witch's spell. They all tried. They all failed.

Then, one day, Grandpapa Rupert whispered in the King's ear what he should do at the wedding of the Prince and Princess. "A good idea, a very good idea indeed," said the King, and instructed his chief courtier to maKe the necessary arrangements.

The Prince and Princess were married in a very unhappy atmosphere and the Princess was still sad as they all sat down for the wedding reception in the big hall.

The King stood up and made his fatherly speech. He turned to his daughter and offered her a present.

Everyone there Knew that the

Princess would guess what the box contained, and they were right.

"Do you Know what the present is?" asked the King, handing his daughter a box with a pretty ribbon tied around it.

"Yes father," said Emilia sadly, "it's a box of chocolates."

"Quite right," said the King, "but the present isn't the box of chocolates - it's the ribbon! A very special ribbon for a very special daughter! A ribbon I had specially made for you."

Instantly, the witch's spell had been broken and Emilia laughed with joy at the surprise. Seeing the Princess laugh, the Prince laughed, the King and Queen laughed and all the courtiers laughed. Everyone was happy and the wedding was perfect.

From now on the Princess was surprised at every present she was given and was blissfully happy that the spell of the Wicked-Witch-of-the-Woods had been broken. She could be surprised and delighted like everyone else, being given a simple gift as well as a more expensive one.

The Prince and Princess Emilia lived happily ever after.

The moral of this story?

Enjoy the surprise of receiving a gift without knowing what it is.

Remember, the surprise is just as important as the gift itself.

And don't wander into dense woods alone when you are only five-years-old or you, too, might meet the Wicked-Witch-of-the-Woods!

GRANDAD'S STORIES

Books forthcoming in this series:

The Seventh Ribbon

~

The Soap Bubble That
Wouldn't Go POP!

~

Peter-the-Shepherdboy

An environmentally friendly booK printed and bound in England by
www.printondemand-worldwide.com

This booK is made entirely of chain-of-custody materials